Gift Aid
462462
50p

D1353985

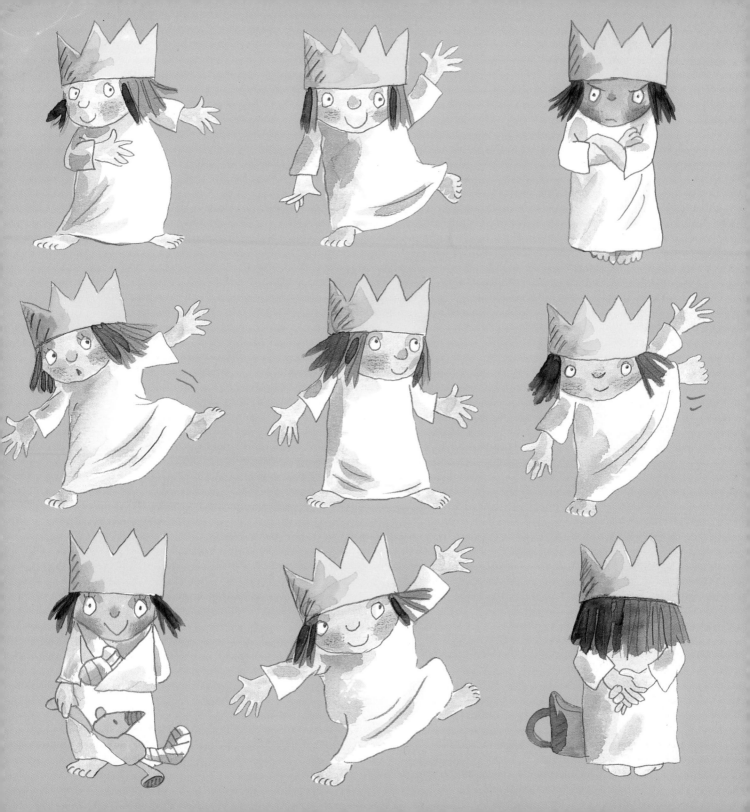

First published in hardback in Great Britain by Andersen Press Ltd in 1995
First published in paperback by Picture Lions in 1996
This edition published by Collins Picture Books in 2001
ISBN-13: 978-0-00-778274-1
ISBN-10: 0-00-778274-8
Picture Lions and Collins Picture Books are imprints of the Children's Division, part of HarperCollins Publishers Ltd.
Text and illustrations copyright © Tony Ross 1995, 2001
The author/illustrator asserts the moral right to be identified as the author/illustrator of the work.
A CIP catalogue record for this title is available from the British Library.

All rights reserved. No part of this publication may be reproduced, stored in a retrieval system or transmitted
in any form or by any means, electronic, mechanical, photocopying, recording or otherwise, without the prior permission of
HarperCollins Publishers Ltd, 77-85 Fulham Palace Road, Hammersmith, London W6 8JB.

Visit our website at: www.harpercollinschildrensbooks.co.uk
Printed in Hong Kong
Colour Reproduction by Dot Gradations Ltd, UK

I Want My Dinner

Tony Ross

Isabel Clark

HarperCollins *Children's Books*

"I WANT MY DINNER!"

"Say PLEASE," said the Queen.

"I want my dinner . . . please."

"Mmmmm, lovely."

"I want my potty."

"Say PLEASE," said the General.

"I want my potty, PLEASE."

"Mmmmm, lovely."

"I want my Teddy . . .

. . . PLEASE," said the Princess.

"Mmmmm."

"We want to go for a walk . . . PLEASE."

"Mmmmm."

"Mmmmm . . . that looks good."

"HEY!" said the Beastie.

"That's MY dinner."

"I want my dinner!"

"Say PLEASE," said the Princess.

"I want my dinner, PLEASE."

"Mmmmm."

"HEY!" said the Princess.

"Say THANK YOU."

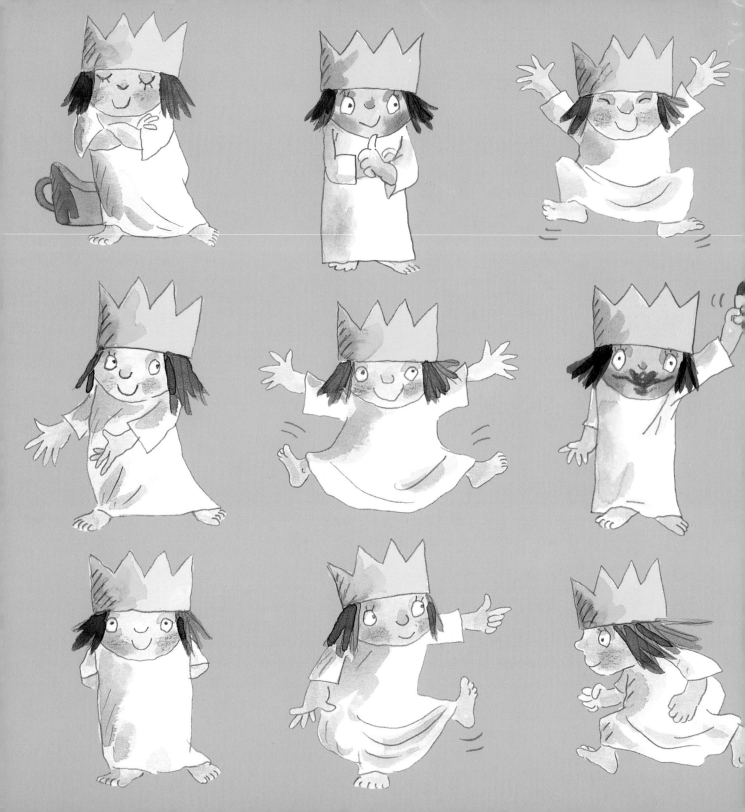

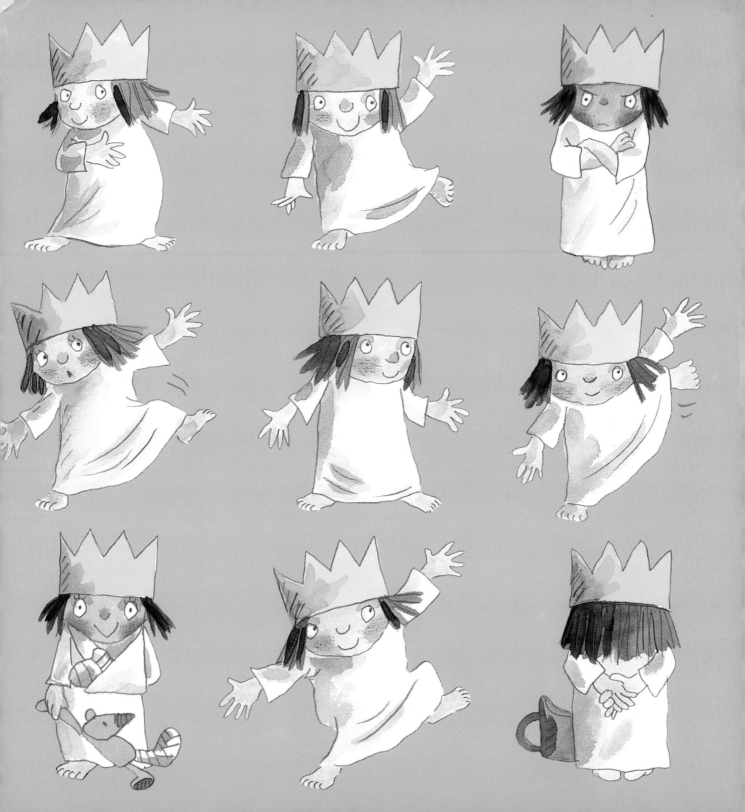